FALCON OF FURY

ADAM BLADE

ORCHARD

MEET TEAM HERO ...

JACK

POWER: Super-strength
LIKES: Ventura City FC
DISLIKES: Bullies

RUBY

POWER: Fire vision
LIKES: Comic books
DISLIKES: Small spaces

DANNY

POWER: Super-hearing and sonic blast
LIKES: Pizza
DISLIKES: Thunder

... AND THEIR GREATEST ENEMY

GENERAL GORE

POWER: Brilliant warrior

LIKES: Carnage

DISLIKES: Unfaithful minions

CONTENTS

QUEEN FELINA led the rulers
of Solus through the great vault
beneath the Solus Pyramid. The dim
chamber was filled with racks of
sunsteel swords, axes and spears,
their keen edges gleaming in the
light of the candles burning on the
stone walls. Chests brimmed with
golden trinkets, and shining suits

of armour hung on stands. Queen
Felina caught a glimpse of her own
lion-like face in a breastplate as she
passed, brow wrinkled in worry.

*Such treasures . . . but no time to
admire them. Not while Solus is in
danger.*

In the middle of the vault, an empty
marble plinth rose up. Queen Felina
headed around it, and stopped in
front of a stone doorway on the far
side of the chamber.

A door that had been closed for a
thousand years.

She approached slowly, her heart
thumping. Behind her, the other

leaders muttered to each other. Placing a paw on the stone door, she pushed. Dust fell from the lintel as it swung open. A warm yellow light flooded out.

Narrowing her eyes, she stepped inside. She gasped.

Beyond was a huge chamber filled with a dazzling pool of gold right in its centre.

Liquid sunsteel.

Great smelters, weapons casts and anvils surrounded the glowing metal lake. Queen Felina turned to the others. "Welcome to the Sunforge," she said.

The light bathed their awed faces
— the scaly snake features of the
Herptamon leader, the stern beak and
feathers of the Avaretti elder, and
the smooth armour of the Tavnar
Scorpion Lord, his stinger glinting
behind him.

"Will we really be able to make a new Starstone?" asked the Herptamon leader, his forked tongue flickering.

Queen Felina sighed. The truth was, she didn't know. Her ancestors had worked this very forge in the first days of Solus. But that was long ago, and most of the secrets of sunsteel smithery had been lost.

"We must try," she said.

Or our whole kingdom will fall . . .

The Starstone that hung over the pyramid had been infected with General Gore's evil spirit. Shadow was spreading over the mini-sun, causing an eclipse to fall slowly over the four cities of Solus. When its poisonous darkness touched the huge guardian statue of each city, the great creatures came to life, under the control of Gore.

The sound of hurried footsteps made them all turn. A woman rushed into the room clutching a yellowing scroll of parchment. She was dressed in a Team Hero uniform, and her purple hair brushed her shoulders as she looked up towards Felina. Felina smiled at the sight of her. Despite the current danger, the queen was so happy to see that her sister was fully recovered from her injuries. For years, Panthera had been a teacher at Hero Academy, calling herself Ms Steel, and using a magic ring to disguise her true Leorian appearance. But she had almost been lost for ever when General Gore's spirit infected her body. "I found it," said Panthera. "The instructions to create a new Starstone."

Queen Felina took the scroll and began to read. The text was ancient Leorian, a language not spoken any more, but which she'd learnt as a girl. "It says here we need a special ingredient to add to the forge," she told the others. "A *Heart of Fire.*"

"What does that mean?" the Scorpion Lord asked Queen Felina, his mouth pincers clicking.

The queen shook her head. "I don't know. It sounds like ancient magic."

The Avaretti elder nodded his beak. "I will instruct our scholars to search our libraries."

"Very good," said Queen Felina, "but hurry."

The bird man nodded, and with a sweep of his robe, marched from the room. The Herptamon and Tavnar leaders began to walk through the forge, staring into the glowing lake. Panthera walked to Queen Felina's side.

"We will find it, I'm sure," said Queen Felina. "Then we will be rid of General

Gore once and for all."

"We must keep hope," agreed her sister. "But there are other concerns." The Hero Academy teacher nodded towards the doorway and Felina followed her out of the forge, back into the vault. Panthera stopped at the huge marble plinth, and stared up at the empty armour rack. Until the day before, it had held the Flameguard, an ancient breastplate and the most powerful of all the artefacts in the vault. It was said to give the wearer power beyond imagining. But it had gone missing. So far the search for it had been in vain.

Queen Felina's fur prickled. "You think it was Gore's minions who took it?" she asked.

Panthera frowned. "In a way, I hope it was Bulk and Smarm. General Gore is a spirit only. Without a body, he cannot wear the Flameguard. Not yet." Panthera paused. "But what if there's a new enemy in our midst? Someone we have yet to discover?"

Queen Felina's gaze snapped up to her sister, her heart sinking with dread. "We do not have the strength to fight two enemies."

Panthera nodded grimly. "Let's just hope we find the armour soon."

CHAPTER 1

CAPTURE THE COBRA

JACK STARED up at Hissrah and felt a shudder. The huge cobra statue, guardian of the Herptamon city, lay coiled on his pedestal. The detail of the carving was incredible — the perfect scaled skin, the head poised to stare out over the city. The snake's neck fanned out and its forked tongue was mid-flicker. Even though it was solid rock, it looked ready to strike at any moment.

And perhaps it soon will . . .

Jack turned from Hissrah towards the Starstone of Solus, a miniature sun that filled the sky above the Great Pyramid at the centre of the kingdom. In times past, it would have thrown life-giving light on each of the four surrounding cities, but now it was just a dimly glowing crescent. The dark section, infected by General Gore's poison, was growing before his eyes, and most of the city of the Herptamon was already cast in shadow. When the tide of black reached Hissrah, the change would be instant. The statue would come to life under General Gore's command.

Jack looked around at the peaceful oases of the snake city, the glistening water channels gliding softly under palm trees, surrounded by brightly painted domes carved from rock. The streets were abandoned except for Solus soldiers. Snake-people clutching knotted whips were ready to defend their city and they were backed up by ranks of winged Avaretti with maces and cat-like Leoriah clad in gleaming armour. Everyone else assembled was from Team Hero — many were students from Hero Academy like Jack and his friends Danny and Ruby. The students were wearing their black skysuits. Their teacher Professor Yokata fiddled nervously with one of the blasters on her hip, drawing, spinning and sliding it back into its holster.

She noticed Jack watching her. "Where *are* they?" she said, checking her watch. "We're running out of time."

"I hear someone coming," said Danny, looking through the trees. Jack could see his friend's bat-like

ears poking through his long hair. All
members of Team Hero had a special
power. Danny's was super-hearing.
Recently, his powers had developed,
and he'd been able to emit a powerful

screech that could deafen opponents.

A few seconds later, several of the Tavnar scorpion-people came scurrying through the trees, dragging behind them a cart creaking under a heavy load.

"Thank goodness they found it," said Ruby, her orange eyes shining.

"Finally," said Yokata. "Right, Team Hero, into position."

They all went to the cart, and began to unfold the sunsteel net that the Solus elders had found in the Pyramid vault. Jack and the others took positions around the net and prepared to move it into place. When

they all had a grip, Professor Yokata
gave the order to rise.

Instead of waiting for the great
statue to come alive, this time Team
Hero planned to be ready and trap the
creature before Gore possessed it.

Jack was used to the flying suit
now. He angled his toes down
slightly and the jet boots
lifted him into the sky.
He carried the
net with him.
Danny wobbled
a little.

"Maybe leave
this to the

experts," said a boy with short black hair, flying opposite. *Olly — of course.* His special power was flight.

"Why are you even wearing a suit?" said Ruby, as she held the net steady.

"Just saving my energy for when the real fight starts," Olly replied.

"Yeah, right," muttered Danny. "Didn't you run away while Jack was busy saving us from Rachnid's poison?"

Olly turned red. "I was cornered by twenty infected Tavnar," he snapped.

"Leave it," said Jack, as Danny opened his mouth to reply.

"Whoops!" said another member of

Team Hero, as he dropped his section of the net. Jack sighed. It was Sam, the new, thin, bony-faced student who kept popping up everywhere. Jack wasn't sure what power he had, but he was certainly clumsy. Somehow he and his large friend, Wendell, who looked like a sumo wrestler, had escaped being injured in the battles so far. Jack spotted the squat new student picking his nose at the base of the statue of Hissrah.

When they had the net ready, they flew up above the statue and released it. The sunsteel strands folded over the stone. The Hero Academy students dropped to the ground and began to tether the net down with giant metal pegs. Jack used his incredible strength to drive them home, his scaled hands glowing.

Suddenly the air beside him shimmered and a dark-skinned woman with purple hair appeared. It was Ms Steel, his teacher from the Academy. The magical golden ring that gave her the appearance of a human glinted on her finger. She stared up at the net draping the statue.

"Nothing will get through that!" said Danny, looking admiringly at the net.

Ms Steel nodded. "I hope you're right."

"Sunsteel is the strongest material in the world," said Ruby. "Even my fire-beams can't melt it." Her eyes flashed briefly, bright as lava.

"It is," replied Ms Steel. "And it is especially strong against shadow. But a trap is only as good as its bait," she added.

What's that supposed to mean? wondered Jack.

"How are things going at the Pyramid?" asked Professor Yokata. She was crouching, checking the tethers on the net.

A fleeting frown passed over Ms Steel's face. "We're getting there," she said. "But creating a new Starstone is not easy."

Jack didn't like the doubt in her voice.

Professor Yokata stood up. "Well, this net should buy us some time," she said. "We're done here. Let's return to HQ."

"See you there," said Ms Steel, and vanished. One by one the students flew into the air, like a swarm of insects taking off.

"Race you!" called Ruby, zooming into the air and flashing a grin back at Danny and Jack.

"Hey! That's not fair," shouted Danny, flying after her.

Jack was still thinking about what Ms Steel had said. Would the leaders of Solus be able to create a new Starstone in time? What would happen if Gore's shadow passed over the entire orb? Would his corrupting shadow spread from Solus, into the rest of the world?

With a sigh, Jack leaped upwards, tilting his boots to activate the jets.

He soared through the hot desert
air, following the others towards the
Solus Pyramid. It was being used as
a temporary base for the battle with
Gore. The Pyramid was stepped, with
fountains and gardens on some of its

levels. And though the huge structure looked completely solid, dozens of rooms both large and small lay within it. The entrance to the inner chambers was on a step between the middle and the top, high above the four cities.

Jack landed and entered through the wide doorway, following a tunnel lit with wall-mounted flaming torches. He could see Ruby and Danny about fifty metres ahead. The rest of the Hero Academy class had already disappeared into the heart of the pyramid with Ms Steel.

Jack was about to call on his

friends to wait, when a hand slipped over his mouth and he felt himself dragged into a side-room. He wrestled himself free and found himself looking at both of the new Team Hero students: large Wendell and bony Sam. The large student slammed the door closed and blocked it.

"What are you doing?" asked Jack. "Is this some sort of joke?" Then he staggered back as something weird began to happen to the two students' features. Their skin seemed to ripple and shift, and Jack gasped as two completely different faces looked back at him. A blotchy one with wide-spaced slabs of teeth peeping over thick lips glistening with spittle, and a gaunt, skeletal one with pale, cold eyes staring from beneath his hood.

These were faces Jack knew all too well.

It was Bulk and Smarm, soldiers of the Noxxian realm, and henchmen of his enemy, General Gore.

"I don't see anyone laughing," said the sorcerer Smarm, his voice a hiss.

CHAPTER 2

TRAITORS WITHIN

HOW COULD I have been such a fool?
Jack thought, his heart thudding.

"Where's the Flameguard, boy?"
snarled the gaunt sorcerer.

Jack frowned, confused.

The ancient armour from the vault?

"I have no idea," he said. His hand
crept towards the hilt on his sunsteel

blade, Blaze, but Bulk grabbed his arm and twisted it painfully behind his back. Jack gritted his teeth.

"You'll tell us, Chosen One," Bulk rumbled. "The boss wants it."

Jack's thoughts whirled. If Gore didn't already have the Flameguard, who *did*?

"I bet he's wearing it under that skysuit," said Smarm. He lifted a hand and his palm crackled with silver sparks. "We can do this the painful way if you want . . . "

"Oh, yes, let's!" Bulk said, grinning horribly.

"You've gone quiet," said Smarm,

moving his hand closer to Jack's face. "But you'll scream for mercy soon."

Jack felt his blood pumping into his scaled hands, his strength growing.

He lifted his legs and kicked Smarm two-footed in the chest, sending him flying back. He ripped his hands from Bulk's hold and shoved him away.

"Catch him!" cried Smarm.

Gore's thug must have weighed three times what Jack did, but the super-strength in Jack's hands sent the henchman crashing through the chamber door and out into the tunnel. Jack jumped over Bulk's prone body and drew Blaze from his side.

Jack heard a crackling sound and
spun round. A bolt of silver energy
shot towards him from Smarm's
hand. Jack lifted his blade, deflecting
the beam. It struck the tunnel ceiling,
making the whole passage rumble.

"What's going on?" yelled Ruby.

Jack saw her and Danny rushing
from the far end of the tunnel. At the
same time he felt pain shoot up his
leg. Bulk had grabbed his ankle with
both his meaty hands. Jack fell to one
knee with a cry.

Bulk began to scrabble at
Jack's skysuit's zip. "Give me the
Flameguard!" he shouted.

Jack delivered a heavy punch to
Bulk's midsection, and the brute fell
back, wheezing for breath.

Smarm walked out into the corridor.
He raised his hands, which were
fizzing with light, and fired a bolt
of magic energy at Ruby. The silver

beam collided with a red one shot from Ruby's eyes, and smoke filled the tunnel. Danny fired a shimmering liquid sunlight bolt at the sorcerer. Smarm's energy beam fizzed out as he threw himself to the side, dodging the bolt, which exploded against the stone wall. The sorcerer screamed at the flash of light. It was the weakness of all Noxxians. Bulk managed to stand, but then he howled as Ruby's eyes sent out a flash of fire that set the back of his trousers alight.

Bulk beat at his clothes frantically with his hands as he ran to Smarm's side, both of them backing towards the exit of the pyramid.

"Not so fast!" said Danny, and fired another crossbow bolt at Smarm.

Jack gasped when the bolt stopped in mid-air and fell to the ground. He realised Smarm had created a barely visible force field. It looked like a glass wall spreading across the tunnel.

"Stalemate," said Smarm, pointed tongue flickering between black teeth.

Breathing hard, Jack rushed forward and swung Blaze at the magical barrier. The blade left spider cracks across the invisible wall, and Smarm's eyes widened. Channelling all the power of his glowing hands, Jack swung again. More cracks. Another blow would destroy it.

Smarm backed away, following Bulk, who was clutching his smoking bottom in pain.

"We must be going now," said the sorcerer. "I probably won't see you again before you all die."

"Big talk, tough guy," said Ruby. "But you can tell Gore we've dealt with the next statue."

Smarm grinned slyly. "You think so? I'm afraid you are mistaken."

Jack drove the point of the sunsteel blade into the forcefield, and it exploded into fragments of shadow.

He ran at Smarm, followed by his friends. He was just a metre short when both their enemies vanished in a burst of red smoke, leaving them alone on the step of the Pyramid.

"Thanks," said Jack to his friends.

They walked to the pyramid exit and gazed out over Solus. The shadow still hadn't reached Hissrah, and the net remained secure over the statue.

Actually, thought Jack, *the shadow's moved further away!*

Dread stole over his skin as he looked back at the Starstone, part shrouded in shadow.

Jack realised that the edge of the

shadow was moving not towards Hissrah, but in the opposite direction. That meant one thing.

Smarm and Bulk must have changed the position of the Starstone! Now the eclipse will fall over the city of the Avaretti and Gore will possess their statue first!

"Hawk," he said, speaking to his Oracle device. "Tell us what the guardian creature of the Avaretti is."

"Her name is Quilla," Hawk replied into his ear. **"An enormous falcon said to keep the weather clement in Solus."**

"The weather isn't looking that *clement* right now," said Ruby, whose

Oracle, Kestrel, had linked to Jack's to hear Hawk's description of Quilla.

Jack stared upwards. A huge magical dome protected Solus from the outside world, but below it, the skies were filling with black clouds that seemed to have come from nowhere. Lightning flashed in their bases. A cold wind whipped sand into his eyes. *Boom!* A crack of thunder rumbled from the sky and crackles of lightning licked the top of the pyramid, causing Jack and his friends to jump back.

Danny pressed his hand to his oracle. "Owl, contact Ms Steel. Tell her to come outside the pyramid, now."

Jack heard Danny's Oracle respond through his own earpiece. *"Unable to connect, Danny. Electrical interference."*

A terrible screech cut through the air, chilling Jack's blood. A shape flew up in front of them, hovering as high as the top of the pyramid. It was a bird of prey — as big as a Team Hero jet. Its tawny feathers glinted at the edges, like sharpened blades. Its fierce beaked face glared coldly down on them. Each beat of its massive wings gusted over Jack's face.

The beak opened, but instead of another bird cry, the rasping voice of

General Gore came out. "Behold my new form, pathetic children," he said. "Your preparations were for nothing. Now I will tear you apart!"

Thunder shook the stone at Jack's feet, just as Quilla steeped her wings and shot towards them.

CHAPTER 3

THE FURY OF QUILLA

"GET BACK!" cried Danny, stepping into the cover of the pyramid corridor with Ruby.

But Jack stepped forward. *I am the Chosen One. I have to fight.* He drew his sword and jumped, his skysuit's jet boots activating. He flew straight towards his enemy.

"No!" cried Ruby, her voice lost in the wind.

Quilla's talons raised, and it reached for Jack. Golden hands glowing, Jack swung Blaze. It crashed into the bird's claws with a shower of sparks, sending the bird flapping to the side. Jack went spinning, out of control, falling towards the ground in dizzying somersaults. He saw the desert sand looming towards him and tried desperately to right himself. But he couldn't stop himself falling. His body screamed with adrenaline. He screwed his eyes shut, just as he was about to hit the ground.

He felt his body jerk upwards as something grabbed him around the middle and hoisted him into the air. Gore had him in the bird's talons, gripped so tightly that Blaze was trapped against Jack's side.

"Don't die yet," said General Gore. "You need to give me the Flameguard first."

The Flameguard? He thinks I have it, too . . .

The giant falcon flapped higher, climbing over the Pyramid of Solus, beneath the shadow-infected Starstone.

"Where is it, Jack?" said General Gore, squeezing his middle so hard

Jack couldn't breathe.

"I . . . don't . . . have it," gasped Jack.

"LIAR!" Gore dipped Quilla's beak and dived towards the city of the Avaretti. Jack saw a city of wide leafy avenues, ornate towers and circular colonnades, with landing platforms on their upper floors. Citizens flapped in panic as they sought to hide. Many of the snake-people of Herptamon were there too, having been evacuated from their own city. They scurried into buildings, or hid behind columns.

"Give it to me!" roared General Gore, his booming voice mingling with a bird-like shriek.

Jack struggled to free his arm, but the grip of the talons was unyielding.

Gore was flying straight towards the tallest of the stone towers which rose from the centre of the city. Jack realised with horror what was about to happen.

"If you won't tell me where the Flameguard is, you're no use at all," said the General.

He flapped Quilla's wings to build up speed, still heading for the tower.

He's going to throw me into it!

"Goodbye, Chosen One," said General Gore.

Jack cried out, his whole body tensing for impact.

A flash of orange light crashed into Quilla's flank, knocking the bird off course. They shot past the tower and Jack missed it by only centimetres.

He turned his head to see Ruby soaring through the air in her skysuit, eyes aglow with power. "Let go of my friend!" she shouted, firing another blast. It ripped across Quilla's feathers, scorching them.

Jack felt the bird's grip loosen and

managed to get one of his hands against a talon. His fingers shone bright gold as he prised himself free. He dropped at once, plummeting towards the stone buildings of the Avaretti city. He kicked out his legs and his jet boots fired, pushing him back up. He hovered above the grand stone towers. Ruby flew towards him, Danny just behind her.

"Are you OK?" asked Danny.

Jack flexed his arms, still throbbing from the vice-like talons. "Just a few bruises. Thanks for coming after me."

They all looked up at Gore, wheeling high above in Quilla's body. Jack

noticed the storm was spreading.
Black clouds swelled in the sky,
massing together. Spots of rain began
to fall.

Gore's cackle filled the air and then
he folded the giant falcon's wings into
a dive. For a moment it looked like

the bird would crash into the ground,
but then Gore levelled out, gliding
along the central avenue of the city.
Sparks of white light crackled along
Quilla's body, and the bird's black
eyes flashed silver.

"Uh-oh," said Danny. "Take cover!"

As soon as he'd said the words, forks of lightning erupted from Quilla's wings, lancing into buildings on either side. Stone cracked apart and walls crumbled into dust. Jack heard cries of fear and pain, as Solus citizens rushed from the falling masonry. The giant falcon careered towards Jack.

"You're in for a shock!" roared General Gore.

More lightning arced from Quilla's feathers, streaming towards Jack. Ruby leapt in front of him, lifting her mirror shield. Jack closed his eyes at a flash of impossibly bright light. He heard a boom and a fizzing sound, then felt Ruby stumble back into him. As he opened his eyes, her shield was ringing like a gong, electricity still spitting from the rim.

The bird's talons latched on to the top of one of the stone towers. Quilla's shriek echoed through the city and the sound sent shivers down Jack's spine.

Danny pointed past where the bird perched. "Is that . . . Olly?"

Jack looked over to where someone in a Team Hero skysuit was rising in the air behind the monstrous falcon, levelling a blaster at the bird's head. "You don't know who you're messing with!" Olly shouted at Gore.

He fired, and the blue energy bolt hit Quilla's beak. The bird let out another shriek, wobbled for a moment, but then righted. The falcon whipped around and flapped, sending a whirlwind at Olly.

"No!" Jack shouted, zooming forward. But it was too late. Olly was thrown against a stone turret. His body went limp as he dropped like a stone on to the slates of the tower's roof.

The falcon's sharp talons scraped the roof, as Gore landed and stalked over to him.

"Hey, bird-brain!" bellowed Danny. "I've got something to tell you!"

Gore turned. Danny opened his mouth wide, letting out a deafening screech which made the air wobble. The

soundwave struck the body of Quilla, sending the giant falcon tumbling to the ground.

"Get Olly," Jack told Ruby. "I'll deal with Gore."

He flew to the edge of the roof. He

expected to find Gore on the other side, lying in a tangle of feathers, but there was no sign of the vast falcon.

Ruby joined him a few moments later with Olly over her shoulder. His eyes were half closed, but Jack was relieved to see he was breathing.

He helped Ruby ease Olly down to the sand and their classmate blinked groggily. Danny landed beside them.

"There!" cried Danny, pointing into the distance.

Beyond the Avaretti city, Jack saw the dark shape of Quilla flapping away through the darkened sky. The bird was approaching the barrier that surrounded Solus, hiding it from the human world. The magical dome was already rippling and weak from the shadow of the Starstone. Gore raised the bird's talons and tore through the barrier. Then he vanished.

"Where's Gore going?" said Ruby.

Dread crept over Jack's chest, as he realised the giant bird had been heading north. It wasn't just empty desert sand that way.

"He's going to Khalea," said Jack, voice shaking. "The human city!"

CHAPTER 4

A CHASE THROUGH THE CLOUDS

"OLLY, STAY here," said Jack. "Tell Professor Yokata and Ms Steel that we're going after Quilla."

The other boy nodded weakly, and Jack sped off with his friends. The buildings of the Avaretti city were a blur beneath him, turning to desert as he reached the outskirts of Solus. He

soared through the hole in the Solus
dome, followed by Ruby and Danny.
Hit with a blazing desert sun, he saw
Quilla's body soaring in the distance.
Beyond was a glittering patch on the
horizon.

Khalea.

Side by side, Jack and his friends
shot across the desert in pursuit
of the creature possessed by the
Noxxian general. Jack didn't even
want to think of the destruction Gore
could cause if he reached the city.
So many innocent lives would be at
stake.

But we're gaining on him . . .

Suddenly Gore flapped Quilla's wings faster, leaving odd spirals of dark cloud in his wake.

"Tornadoes!" shouted Ruby, over the sudden roar of wind. The cyclones twisted towards them — five, ten, twenty of them. Jack veered under one, and felt himself sucked towards another. Only by blasting his thrusters did he escape its deadly pull. Ruby was zipping back and forth through an obstacle course of spinning clouds.

"Whoa!" Danny screamed.

Jack looked back to see Danny being whipped through a spiral of

whipping wind. Jack zoomed over and pulled his friend from the twister.

"Thanks!" said Danny, eyes wide.

"Come on," called Ruby. "Gore's getting away."

They flew on and reached the villages on the outskirts of the city,

where wide water channels cut
through the desert, bringing life
to vast swathes of farmland. Here
and there small villages dotted the
pastures. Gore flew lower, and sparks
of lightning brewed in the giant
falcon's wings. Workers in the fields
stared up in horror.

As lightning bolts streaked to the
ground, the farmers began to scream
and run. Fires sprang up in the
fields, and bitter smoke trailed in
the sky. Then Gore moved on to the
farmhouses. One by one Gore torched
them with his deadly power. Jack lost
sight of Quilla's shape in the black

clouds of ash and smoke.

"Behold what I can do!" came Gore's booming voice. "And soon, your whole world will face the same fate."

"Your skysuit is low on power," said Hawk suddenly in Jack's ear. *"It will deactivate in ten minutes."*

"Great. Just what I need," said Jack. He climbed higher, above the smoke, and saw Gore heading towards the soaring steel and glass skyscrapers of Khalea. "This way!" he shouted to Danny and Ruby.

The great bird swooped and tipped on to its side, slaloming between tall buildings. Jack imagined the stories on the news. *Giant bird attacks city*. There was no way Team Hero would be able to cover this up, was there?

"Split up!" said Jack, through his Oracle. "We have to intercept Gore."

They broke apart, Ruby and Danny taking the flanks, while Jack flew at Quilla's tail, threading between more towers. As his friends looped in from either side, Ruby shot a fire-beam and Danny shot a bolt from his crossbow. Quilla's sharp, falcon eyes must have spotted them. With a sudden flex of its wings, the living statue rose above both shots, and then flapped its wings with a shriek. Two tornadoes headed towards Jack's friends.

Danny managed to dodge, but Ruby wasn't so lucky. The twister knocked her off course. Jack saw her spiralling towards the ground, caught in the grip of the spinning wind. A ripple of fear passed down his neck, and he zoomed forwards in a steep dive. He entered the tornado and grabbed Ruby around the waist, tugging at her with his super-strength. They flew out from the other side.

"Guys!" said Danny through their Oracles. "Quick! I need you here."

Jack looked around, but his friend and Gore were nowhere to be seen.

"Hawk, show me Danny's position."

"Rendering map, Jack," came the response in his ear.

Jack saw Danny appear as a dot on his visor. He flew towards it, zipping low over the ground above the heads of amazed onlookers. They shot under a monorail, and then up over a street market, reaching the river that flowed through Khalea. A fierce wind was whipping up, created by Quilla. Pleasure boats, large and small, were dotted across the river, rolling in the swirling water. But one particular cruise ship caught Jack's attention. The huge vessel was rocking dangerously back and forth, as Gore buffeted it with huge flaps of Quilla's wings. On the deck, passengers clung to the rails and each other in fear.

"Gore's trying to tip it!" called Danny from above them. "What do we do?"

As the ship rolled, the first passenger fell from the side with a cry and entered the water. Then another.

"Try to keep him busy," said Jack. "We need to save these people!"

"I'm on it!" said Ruby.

Twin bursts of flame from her eyes scorched the air, but Gore must have seen them coming, because Quilla's body twisted away. At the same time,

the ship lurched, spilling dozens of people into the water.

"There are still people trapped inside!" cried Danny. "They'll drown!"

General Gore laughed, as the giant falcon rose into the air. "Sorry, heroes. There's nothing you can do this time."

"Help those in the water!" Jack said.

"What about the ones on the ship?" asked Danny.

"I've got an idea!" said Jack. He flew down to the edge of the tipping vessel. He pushed his palms against the side of the leaning boat and cranked his jet boots to full power. *What if I can't do it? What if I let these people die?*

"You can do it, Jack!" called Ruby. She was lifting a small boy from the water while Danny was rowing a boat from the shore towards others stranded in the water.

Jack gritted his teeth. He pushed up with his arms, elbows shaking. Slowly,

the boat began to move, rising slightly. He roared in pain, as his shoulders burned with effort. His hands felt almost aflame. With one powerful heave, he threw the side of the boat upwards. The boat sloshed upright in the river, water flowing off the deck.

I did it!

The passengers cheered. On deck they tossed lifebuoys to those still in the water. Danny and Ruby were helping people on to the bank of the river. Danny grinned at Jack, and Ruby gave him a thumbs-up.

"Nice work, Chosen One," she said through her Oracle.

Jack heard a squawk. Looking up, he saw Quilla's dark shape disappearing through the clouds. Jack kicked and repositioned his legs to give chase, but a second later the jets spluttered, and Jack dropped a metre or so before the boots fired again.

"I'm afraid your suit is out of power," said Hawk.

Jack's heart sank as he watched the bird flapping away.

There was nothing he could do to stop General Gore.

CHAPTER 5

AIR EMERGENCY

JACK FLEW towards the shore, dropping and rising as his boots failed. Finally, the jets cut out completely and he crashed down on to the muddy bank, next to Ruby and Danny.

Hope drained from Jack as Gore disappeared over the horizon.

Jack felt a tremendous rush of
wind but he couldn't tell where it was
coming from. Then the air above the
river blurred like a mirage and a huge
shape appeared — a sleek black plane.

"It's Arrow!" said Danny.

A large hatch in the bottom of the
Team Hero jet plane opened and
Professor Yokata leaned out. "Need a

ride?" she said.

Ropes fell from the opening and Danny, Ruby and Jack hooked themselves on by their belt harnesses. Winches pulled them up into the body of the craft. On the deck of the cruise ship below, citizens of Khalea pointed and waved.

The hatch closed and Jack unhitched the rope buckle. Apart from the Professor, the only other person on board was Olly, slouched on the bench, looking pale but uninjured. Jack quickly shrugged off his skysuit and put on a fresh, full-powered one.

"Can we take down General Gore with

Arrow?" Jack asked Professor Yokata.

"That's the plan," she replied, slipping into the pilot seat and turning off autopilot. "Jack, I need you and Ruby on weapons. Danny, listen out for Quilla."

They took their positions, Danny up front beside their teacher, and Ruby and Jack on opposite sides of the cockpit, clutching the missile blasters. Olly looked on, jaw clenched.

Yokata pushed the throttle and the plane zoomed upwards, taking them above the highest skyscrapers of central Khalea.

Lightning flashed through the

bellies of the clouds, rocking Arrow. A downpour of rain cascaded over the windscreen.

"That way!" said Danny, pointing to the port side.

Jack felt himself pressed back in the seat as Arrow accelerated into the desert. Through gaps in the cloud, he saw Quilla flying below them. He focused on the target monitor, letting the crosshairs settle over the huge falcon. He'd had some lessons with aircraft weaponry — but the years spent playing his computer console were the real training. "Locking on," he said, and then: "Firing!"

As he pulled the trigger, the craft shook wildly and tipped sideways. Sparks crackled across the controls. Jack watched his missile trail wide, exploding into the desert floor.

"There's too much lightning," said Yokata. "We have to descend."

As she did, Jack saw the dome surrounding Solus spread out below. The magical barrier that shrouded Solus from the outside world was usually invisible, but Jack saw where Quilla had ripped a large new hole in it. The massive falcon must have damaged the barrier's ability to hide and protect the secret cities.

Gore's gone back to Solus.

"Look out!" called Ruby.

Jack saw the tornado dead ahead and knew it was too late. The twister was fifty metres across. The whole craft creaked and shook as the tornado

enveloped it, hurling Jack and the others out of their seats. He smashed into the ceiling, then into Danny. Alarms and beeps went off all around as Arrow spun in freefall. Dials and displays were going haywire.

"Abandon ship!" yelled Professor Yokata. Her head was bleeding where she'd crashed into something.

Jack grabbed the wall and fumbled his way along into the fuselage, grabbing hold of Danny on the way. "Form a chain!" he said. "Olly, open the hatch!"

Bouncing around, Olly managed to press the release button and the floor-hatch slid open. Through it, Jack saw sand rushing to meet them. The altimeter siren was blaring loudly. *How long before we hit the ground?*

He reached the edge of the hatch and hurled himself out, tensing his legs to switch on the jet boots. He slowed his fall, but not enough. He flung out his arms and slammed into a dune, rolling down the side and sliding to a stop at the base. A moment later he heard a tremendous explosion.

Jack spat out a mouthful of sand and wiped his face. Flames and billowing smoke climbed into the sky a couple of hundred metres away, from the wreckage of the Team Hero craft. His heart jolted.

Where are my friends? Did they make it?

He realised the jet had fallen straight through the hole in Solus's magical dome to crash on the edge of the Herptamon city. Brightly coloured stone buildings were ahead, along with streams and lush oases. Jack stood on trembling legs and turned in a circle. *There!* Ruby, Danny, and Olly were picking themselves up from the sand. *But what about Professor Yokata? Was she still trapped inside Arrow when it crashed?*

He rushed towards the others,
but halfway there he stumbled over
something half-buried — an arm. He
fell to his knees and dug at the sand.
The others reached his side and did
the same. Soon they'd uncovered their
teacher. She was face down. Jack
rolled her over, fearing the worst.

Professor Yokata smiled
weakly, and Jack's
heart leapt with joy.

"Where's . . . Gore?"
Yokata said.

Jack scanned the
sky, and saw Quilla
perched on the peak of

the Solus Pyramid. "Can you move?" he asked the Professor.

Yokata shook her head. "I think my leg is broken," she said, grimacing.

"We'll get help," said Ruby, standing up, but Yokata caught her ankle.

"Not until we've dealt with our enemy," she said. "That's an order."

Ruby's brow wrinkled with worry, but she nodded.

"How can we stop Gore?" said Danny, hands on his knees and breathing heavily.

Jack tried to stay calm. As he cleared his mind his eyes fell on the snake statue, swathed in the sunsteel net. He remembered Ms Steel's strange words, before Quilla became possessed by Gore.

A trap is only as good as its bait . . .

He smiled grimly. *Perhaps there is a way.*

"Come with me," he said to the others. "I've got an idea."

"Good luck," said Professor Yokata.

Jack led the others to the Herptamon statue.

"Why are we going this way?" said Olly. "We need to go after General Gore. In case you hadn't noticed, he's in the other direction!"

"We need to use the sunsteel net to

ensnare him," said Jack, staying calm.

"Er . . . I'm not sure Gore will fall for that," said Danny. "What makes you think he'll come anywhere near it?"

"Because I'll be the bait," said Jack.

Ruby's eyes bore into Jack. "Are you sure this is a good idea?" she asked.

Jack tried to look confident. "General Gore wants the Flameguard, right? Well, he thinks I have it."

The others nodded. "It might work," said Danny. "But if it doesn't, you're as good as dead."

Hearing that, Jack began to have doubts. "Just be ready," he said.

They pulled out the posts holding

down the net, then Jack rose in his skysuit, before zooming towards the Pyramid where Quilla was perched. It wasn't long before General Gore spotted him.

"You never learn," Gore said. "Will I have to kill you all?"

"Just me," said Jack. "If you want the Flameguard."

"I knew you had it!" said Gore, spreading Quilla's wings, and launching from the peak.

"You'll have to catch me first, though," Jack shouted. He wheeled away and flew towards the bird city of the Avaretti.

CHAPTER 6

BAITING THE TRAP

AT ONCE Jack realised Quilla was far quicker than him in the air. The bird's black eyes fixed on him with hate as she gained on him. Jack descended towards the towers of the Avaretti city itself. *I'll be safer on the ground, among the buildings . . .* He couldn't see his friends, but had to trust they'd made it ahead of him.

He landed and broke into a run, slipping down a narrow alley. A flash of Quilla's lightning cracked into the building at his side, showering rubble and ash across him. He kept running, and took another turn. Quilla's shadow passed overhead.

"Run, little one," called Gore, "but soon your legs will tire."

Jack's chest was already heaving with the effort of sprinting in the skysuit. Scaled and beaked faces peered from Avaretti homes as he rushed past. A buffeting gale hit him full in the front, knocking him on to his back. He saw Gore had managed to get ahead, beating Quilla's wings madly. He scrambled up, but another blast threw him into a double door, smashing it from its hinges. He found himself on the floor of a grand stone chamber, groaning. His plan was in tatters already.

The chamber was dimly lit by ornate glass lanterns. Tall shelves lined two walls, packed with scrolls, and there were murals on the walls painted in natural colours — green, ochres, reds and yellow. It was some sort of museum or library. He picked himself up and dusted himself down, wondering if there was another door. He crossed the room, and his eyes were drawn to pictures painted across the stone walls. It looked like some sort of battle between the people of Solus and another army. Jack recognised the familiar shapes of centipede soldiers and skeleton warriors. *This must be a scene of Solus citizens fighting the Noxxians during General Gore's first invasion!*

There was no other exit from the chamber, so Jack hurried back towards the door he'd crashed through, listening out for sounds of Quilla's wings.

Lightning struck the threshold, and Jack shielded his eyes from the flying sparks.

"Come out, Jack," bellowed Gore. "Give me the Flameguard and I will let you live."

The contempt in the General's voice filled Jack with determination. He stood, picked up the huge fallen door like a shield and ran out into the street. Electric bolts fizzed at him from Quilla's wings but Jack raised his makeshift shield, blocking the jolts of lightning. His hands glowed gold, filling with strength and he hurled the slab of wood into the sky.

It caught Gore on the chest, and the bird's wings flailed as the great falcon fell back.

Jack activated his jet boots and flew to the city's main avenue. His chest flooded with relief as he saw Quilla's empty plinth looming ahead. But were the others in position? He wouldn't know until the crucial moment.

"You'll pay for that!" cried General Gore.

Jack looked over his shoulder and saw the terrifying sight of Quilla close on his tail. As Jack turned back he saw another flying shape zoom towards him, flying into formation at his side.

"Olly!" Jack said, startled. "You should be with Ruby and Danny!"

"And let you get all the credit again?" said Olly. "Forget it!" He looked back at Gore. "You'll never have the Flameguard!" he shouted.

But he wasn't watching where he was flying and knocked into Jack, sending him off course.

"Careful!" cried Jack, righting himself.

"That was your fault!" said Olly.

Jack saw Quilla's lightning flicker across its wings. "Olly, look out!"

No sooner had the words left his mouth than a fork of lightning lit up the air around them. In a flash he saw it strike Olly, bursting into a fireball against his chest. His fellow student screamed and careered from the sky, crashing to the ground. Speechless, Jack flew on in horror. *No one could survive that blast. He's dead — he has to be.*

"You're next, Jack!" said Gore. He fired another bolt, and Jack dodged sideways. The streak of lightning hit the plinth in front of Jack, sending cracks through the stone.

Still in shock, Jack tried to stay focused on the plan. He flew towards the plinth. Gore came after him, his laughter filling the air. As Jack passed over the plinth, he saw Ruby and Danny crouching on the other side, holding the net ready.

"Now!" he shouted.

Their jet boots fired and they shot
upwards, raising the net in front
of Gore. He tried to swerve but too
late. The giant falcon plunged right
into the waiting net, which tangled
around Quilla's body, and was ripped
from Ruby and Danny's hands. The
squirming, feathered shape crashed to
the sand, writhing, but unable to break
free from the golden net. Jack flew
down with his sword ready.

But something odd was already
happening. Quilla's feathers were
changing colour, a grey pallor creeping

over the brown feathers. As it did, they seemed to stiffen. Gore's strangled cry came from within the net. "This is not the end, Jack. I will have the Flameguard and take over your world. My shadow will sprea—"

The voice went silent as Quilla's body hardened to stone.

"What happened?" asked Danny, landing alongside Jack.

"It must have been the sunsteel in the net," said Ruby, still floating above. She glanced around. "Where's Olly? He said he was coming to help you."

Jack looked at the ground, icy cold stabbing inside his stomach. *How can I tell them what happened?*

"Jack?" said Danny.

It's my fault, thought Jack. *I should've saved him.* "He's dead," he whispered. "General Gore killed him with a lightning bolt."

"You're not talking about me, are you?" said a voice.

Jack spun round to see Olly, drifting towards them. His skysuit was half melted away, but otherwise he was fine. He was actually smiling.

"That's impossible!" said Jack. "I saw the flames. I saw you crash."

Olly shrugged. "Guess I'm tougher than I look," he said.

Then Jack noticed he was wearing something under his damaged skysuit — something silver with red edging.

"Olly, that's the Flameguard!" Jack said. "It protected you!"

"*You're* the thief!" cried Danny.

Olly blushed as he looked down, then tried to cover up with his arms.

"Why do you have it?" asked Ruby.

Olly's face took on a different look — wild and fierce. His eyes flashed with defiance. "Because I earned it!" he snapped.

"It belongs to Solus!" said Danny. "Take it off."

"No chance," replied Olly. He spun

in the air and shot away. "With this armour I will be the greatest hero ever!"

Jack was about to chase after his classmate when he heard pounding footsteps. It was Ms Steel, Queen Felina and the other Solus leaders, all rushing towards them. Some stopped to gaze up at the petrified form of Quilla, still covered in the sunsteel net.

The Avaretti ruler ruffled his feathers and nodded solemnly. "Team Hero has saved us again."

Jack gazed around at the Avaretti city, half of which had been set on fire by Quilla's lightning. It didn't feel much like a victory.

He wondered if he should tell them about the Flameguard, but decided to wait until he'd talked with Ms Steel in private.

Queen Felina looked grave. She pointed to the Starstone. "We are beginning to run out of time," she said. The shadow now covered almost all of the mini-sun. Nearly the entire valley of Solus was shrouded in darkness.

Jack clenched his fists. "We won't give up." He looked at his friends, and saw they too had their heads held high. Team Hero would stick by one another always.

And together, we will triumph.

n't called Hero Force yet, but they soon would

...led by Gretchen of Ventura, a young

TIMETABLE

	MON	TUE	WED	THUR	FRI
	ASSEMBLY	ASSEMBLY	ASSEMBLY	ASSEMBLY	ASSEMBLY
08.00	POWERS	POWERS	POWERS	POWERS	POWERS
09.00	COMBAT	STRATEGY	TECH	COMBAT	STRATEGY
10.00	MATHS	GEOGRAPHY	ENGLISH	HISTORY	ENGLISH
11.00	HISTORY	SCIENCE	MATHS	SCIENCE	GEOGRAPHY
12.00					
13.00			LUNCH!		
14.00	TECH	COMBAT	COMBAT	STRATEGY	WEAPON TRAINING
15.00	GYM	GYM	WEAPON TRAINING	GYM	GYM
16.00	GYM	GYM	GYM	GYM	HOMEWORK
17.00	HOMEWORK	HOMEWORK	HOMEWORK	HOMEWORK	FREE

HOMEWORK

TECH: CREATE A SIMULATED
SUNLIGHT CIRCUIT

ENGLISH: WRITE A POEM
ABOUT THE IMPORTANCE OF
DISCIPLINE IN TRAINING

SCIENCE: LIST THE
FIVE MOST EXPLOSIVE
NOXXIAN ELEMENTS

TEAM HERO ACADEMY

READ ON FOR A SNEAK
PEEK AT BOOK 8:

RISE OF THE SHADOW
SNAKES

CHAPTER 1

HISSRAH

THIS PLACE should be a paradise, thought Jack, gazing around at the Herptamon city. Painted domes, ringed with coiling terraces, spread out among the leafy oasis. The air was filled with the scent of flowers and ripe fruit.

But a cold wind blew among the

trees, and foliage that should have
been vivid green was cast in shade.
Jack stared at the Starstone, floating
over the Great Pyramid in the middle
of Solus. Once it had blazed, throwing
a golden glow over the four cities.
Now it was almost entirely infected by
the shadow of General Gore. Only a
sliver of light remained, and Jack let it
bathe his face.

It might be the last time I ever feel it.

For days he'd watched the shadow
growing, despair creeping over his
heart. If they didn't stop it soon, and
the blackness took over completely,
it wasn't just the four cities of Solus

that would suffer. There'd be nothing to prevent Gore's shadow infecting the entire world.

Ruby's voice spoke through Hawk, the Oracle device in his ear.

"We don't have long, Jack. How's it going?"

CHECK OUT BOOK EIGHT: RISE OF THE SHADOW SNAKES to find out what happens next!

IN EVERY BOOK OF
TEAM HERO SERIES
ONE there is a special
Power Token. Collect
all four tokens to get
an exclusive Team Hero
Club pack. The pack
contains everything you and
your friends need to form your
very own Team Hero Club.

MEMBERSHIP CARDS · MEMBERSHIP CERTIFICATE · STICKERS · POWER GAME · BOOKMARKS

Just fill in the form below, send it in with your four tokens
and we'll send you your Team Hero Club Pack.

SEND TO: Team Hero Club Pack Offer, Hachette Children's Books,
Marketing Department, Carmelite House, 50 Victoria Embankment,
London, EC4Y 0DZ.

CLOSING DATE: 31st December 2018

WWW.TEAMHEROBOOKS.CO.UK

Please complete using capital letters *(UK and Republic of Ireland residents only)*

FIRST NAME

SURNAME

DATE OF BIRTH

ADDRESS LINE 1

ADDRESS LINE 2

ADDRESS LINE 3

POSTCODE

PARENT OR GUARDIAN'S EMAIL

I'd like to receive Team Hero email newsletters and information about
other great Hachette Children's Group offers (I can unsubscribe at any time)

*Terms and conditions apply. For full terms and conditions please go to
teamherobooks.co.uk/terms*

*TEAM HERO Club packs
available while stocks last.
Terms and conditions apply.*

COLLECT ALL OF SERIES TWO!

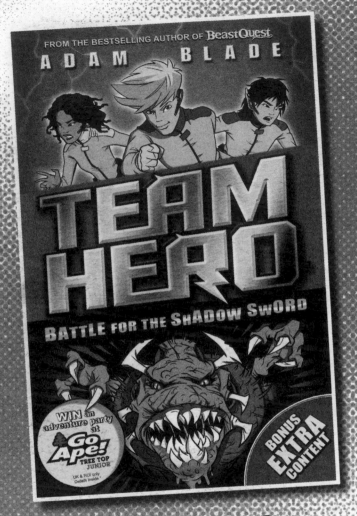